Other Books by
Irma Simonton Black
Published by Albert Whitman

ॐ

THE LITTLE OLD MAN
WHO COULD NOT READ

THE LITTLE OLD MAN
WHO COOKED AND CLEANED

DOCTOR PROCTOR
and MRS. MERRIWETHER

Story by Irma Simonton Black
Pictures by Leonard Weisgard

ALBERT WHITMAN *& Company*
Chicago

Standard Book Number: 8075–1654–6
L. C. Catalog Card: 78–150800
Text © 1971 by Irma Simonton Black
Illustrations © 1971 by Leonard Weisgard
Published simultaneously in Canada by
George J. McLeod, Limited, Toronto
Lithographed in U.S.A.

Susan! Susan!"
Peter Coles called.

"I'm not Susan,"
his sister Susan called back.
"I'm Mrs. Merriwether.
And I have a sick baby."

So Mrs. Merriwether
(who was Susan) turned to
her baby Celeste.

"Oh dear, oh dear, Celeste,
please eat this," she said.
  But
Celeste would not eat.

"Mrs. Merriwether," Peter called.

"Yes," said his sister Susan.

"You should ask the doctor to look
at your baby, Mrs. Merriwether," he said.

"Yes," said his sister Susan again.
"I'll call the doctor right now."

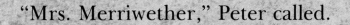

Mrs. Merriwether reached over
to put ten blankets on Celeste *but*
her foot pressed so hard on the rocker
of Celeste's cradle that

PLOP!

Celeste rolled out
and fell flat on the floor.

Right on her face!
And she had a scratch.

"Oh dear, now you're hurt and sick too,"
said Susan. "Peter, Peter, come quick!"

But—

"I'm not Peter," her brother Peter said.
"I'm Doctor Proctor."

"How wonderful," said his sister Susan.
"Doctor Proctor, come quick!"

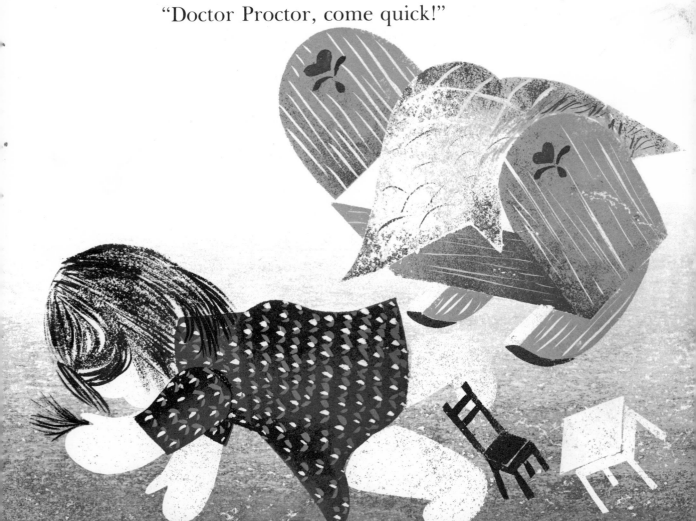

Doctor Proctor (who was Peter, of course)
ran to the shelf and got his doctor's bag.

Then he ran to Susan's house.
"Bzzzz" he went, just like a doorbell.

Mrs. Merriwether said,
"Oh, Doctor Proctor, I'm so glad to see you.
Come right in."

"Where is the patient?" Doctor Proctor asked.
"What seems to be the trouble?"

"Right here," said Mrs. Merriwether.
"She fell out of her cradle and hurt herself—
and she already had a cold and a chill."

"That's a big scratch," said Doctor Proctor.
"Have you put medicine on it?"

"Oh no," said Mrs. Merriwether.
"I wanted you to see it first."

Doctor Proctor opened his bag.
He took out a little bottle
with a glass stopper.
Carefully he put some pink medicine
on the scratch.

"Aren't you going to bandage it?"
asked Mrs. Merriwether.
"Celeste loves bandages.
I did too when I was little."

"So did I," said Doctor Proctor.
"But I want to examine her
before I put the bandage on."

"Of course," said Mrs. Merriwether.

Doctor Proctor sat down by Celeste
and put her on her stomach.
  but
Celeste made a crying sound.

"Now, Celeste, it's all right," said Mrs. Merriwether.
"You know Doctor Proctor is your friend.
My doctor was my friend when I was a little girl.
He'll make you all well."

Celeste didn't say one word.

Doctor Proctor sat Celeste up
and took Celeste's wrist
in his hand.
She didn't cry.
Then he said, "Pulse OK."

He pulled out a tiny tongue depressor
and looked in her mouth as far as he could.

"Wider," said Mrs. Merriwether.
"Celeste, open your mouth the way
I used to do when I was a little girl."

"It's fine," said Doctor Proctor.
"I can see enough.
Just a little sore throat."

Then Doctor Proctor got out a little light
to look in Celeste's ears.
"Good," he said. "Nothing wrong there."

"Oh, oh, I think she's going to cry again,"
said Mrs. Merriwether. "Celeste dear,
Doctor Proctor needs you to blow out
his little light."

Celeste didn't blow, of course,
so Mrs. Merriwether puffed at the little light
and it went out.
(That was because Peter turned it off.)

"I used to love to do that when I was little,"
she said to Doctor Proctor.

"I did too," he said.

Doctor Proctor took out his stethoscope
and listened to Celeste's chest.

"Fine and thumpy," he said.
"Now I'll have another look at that scratch."

Mrs. Merriwether waited as Doctor Proctor asked,
"Celeste, would you like a round bandage
or a square one?" *But* Celeste did not answer.

"I always liked the round bandage when
I was little," said Mrs. Merriwether.

So Celeste got the round bandage
to cover her scratch.

"Now a pill for her sore pink throat,"
Doctor Proctor said. "Here, Celeste,
they taste just like candy."

(Doctor Proctor's pills really were candy—
because he was a play doctor.)

He put a pink pill in Celeste's mouth
but she didn't take it, so he ate it himself.

"Let me try to give it to her," said Mrs. Merriwether.

But Celeste didn't take the pill from her,
      so Mrs. Merriwether had to eat it herself.

"Yum," she said. "Celeste needs more."
                        But —

"Stop!" said Doctor Proctor.
"You'll eat up too much of my medicine.
My goodness! I almost forgot Celeste's shot."

Doctor Proctor took his hypodermic needle
and pressed it against Celeste's arm.
"Don't cry, Celeste," the doctor said.
"It's like a little mosquito bite."

"Yes, don't cry," said Mrs. Merriwether.
"I never cried when I was little."
So Celeste didn't cry.

"That's it," said Doctor Proctor. "All done.
Give her lots of juices and lots of rest.
Call me tomorrow."

Then Peter left, and
Mrs. Merriwether put Celeste back
in her cradle and rocked her.

Mrs. Merriwether looked up and saw
her brother Peter out in the yard.
He wasn't Doctor Proctor any more—
he was climbing a tree.

Mrs. Merriwether went to the window
and opened it.

"Hey, Mrs. Merriwether!" Peter called.
"Come on out."

But —

"I'm not Mrs. Merriwether anymore,"
his sister said.
"I'm Susan Coles,
and I'm coming out right now."

In encounter groups and sensitivity sessions, adults use a method children naturally employ to recreate significant experiences: dramatic play. While acting out the roles of mother and doctor is a game on one level, Irma Simonton Black shows that on a deeper level it is a way of reassuring oneself that "If I'm sick, I'll be looked after by people who love me."

Irma Simonton Black has written more than twenty picture books, but this is only one side of her career. She has taught children's literature, worked with parents, and through her association with the Bank Street School of Education in New York City she has had an important responsibility for making children's reading materials reflect the urban scene. As Senior Editor in charge of Bank Street publications, she has guided preparation of a primary reading series published by Macmillan and intermediate books put out by Houghton Mifflin.

When Mrs. Black talks about her own books, she recalls the challenge and delight of working with Lucy Sprague Mitchell. Mrs. Mitchell saw the everyday context of children's lives as story material. This seems so self-evident now that its novelty when Mrs. Mitchell commenced to write is often forgotten.

A picture book is, of course, the creative effort of two people. When Mrs. Black showed her manuscript about Doctor Proctor and Mrs. Merriwether to Leonard Weisgard, he agreed to illustrate it. Time intervened, and no one foresaw that when the book was ready for publication Mr. Weisgard would be living in Denmark. This proved no bar, however, to a happy collaboration.

Leonard Weisgard is American born and won the Caldecott medal in 1947 for *The Little Island* by Golden McDonald, pseudonym for Margaret Wise Brown. He has created many lovely picture books for children and has written and illustrated a number of his own. Color, pattern, and mood each play a part in making the books he illustrates ones children like to look at over and over.